Kelp's Wish Upon Three Moons

Adapted by Patty Michaels

Based on the original book by Jessie Sima

SIMON SPOTLIGHT · An imprint of Simon & Schuster Children's Publishing Division
New York   London   Toronto   Sydney   New Delhi
1230 Avenue of the Americas, New York, New York 10020 · This Simon Spotlight edition August 2024
DreamWorks Not Quite Narwhal © 2024 DreamWorks Animation LLC. All Rights Reserved. All rights reserved, including the right of
reproduction in whole or in part in any form. **SIMON SPOTLIGHT** and colophon are registered trademarks of Simon & Schuster, LLC.
Simon & Schuster: Celebrating 100 Years of Publishing in 2024 · For information about special discounts for bulk purchases,
please contact Simon & Schuster Special Sales at 1-866-506-1949 or business@simonandschuster.com.
Manufactured in China 0424 SCP 10 9 8 7 6 5 4 3 2 1
ISBN 978-1-6659-6095-3 · ISBN 978-1-6659-6096-0 (ebook)

Kelp was excited to go to Unicorn Land for his first-ever Three Moon Festival!

"Why can't the festival be in the ocean?" Scallop asked sadly.

Kelp wanted to cheer up Scallop. "How about before I go, I make you a bubble necklace?" he offered.

"I just love it," Scallop said, admiring her beautiful necklace.

Scallop swam with Kelp to the ocean's surface. On their way Cruz spotted them.

"What are you all dressed up for?" Cruz asked. In his hair Kelp wore his favorite fancy clip that Scallop had given to him!

"I'm going to my first Three Moon Festival up on Unicorn Land!" Kelp said.

"And I'm escorting him," Scallop added.

"Are you going to show off your dance moves?" Cruz asked.

Kelp twirled and shimmied as Cruz and Scallop cheered him on.

"You're glowing!" Cruz exclaimed.

Kelp looked down. "I am glowing!" he realized.

"It's the plankton," Scallop told them. "It glows sometimes. **The ocean has magic, too!**"

When they reached the surface of the ocean, Scallop and Cruz waved goodbye to Kelp.
"I wish I was going to a festival," Scallop said.
"Me too," Cruz agreed.

When Kelp arrived at the festival, he couldn't believe his eyes. The unicorns were creating globes of sparkly lights with their Unicorn Spark! "Wow! What are these glowing things?" Kelp wondered.

He overheard his friend Pixie call them **wish lanterns.**

Ollie ran over to Kelp and admired his rainbow clip. "It's perfect for your first Three Moon Festival," Ollie told him.

"Why is it called Three Moon Festival?" Kelp asked.

"Because it's the one time of year where we get to see three moons in the night sky!" Ollie exclaimed.

Ollie and Kelp stared up at the wish lantern Ollie made with his Unicorn Spark. "Wow!" Kelp said. Just then, Juniper's sparkling green wish lantern flew toward them.

"Oops," Juniper said. She was still learning how to make wish lanterns.
"Sorry," Pixie said. "Juniper is having a little trouble with her wish lantern."

"Juni, you need to focus on the three moons," Pixie told her. "Imagine them in the sky. And then, the three moons inside your wish lantern will guide your wish smoothly to the moons! Just like this."

Pixie tried to send her wish lantern to the three moons, but when it reached the clouds, the fog pushed it back to her.

"**Oh no!**" Ollie cried. "It's fog. And it is not good. Not for today!"

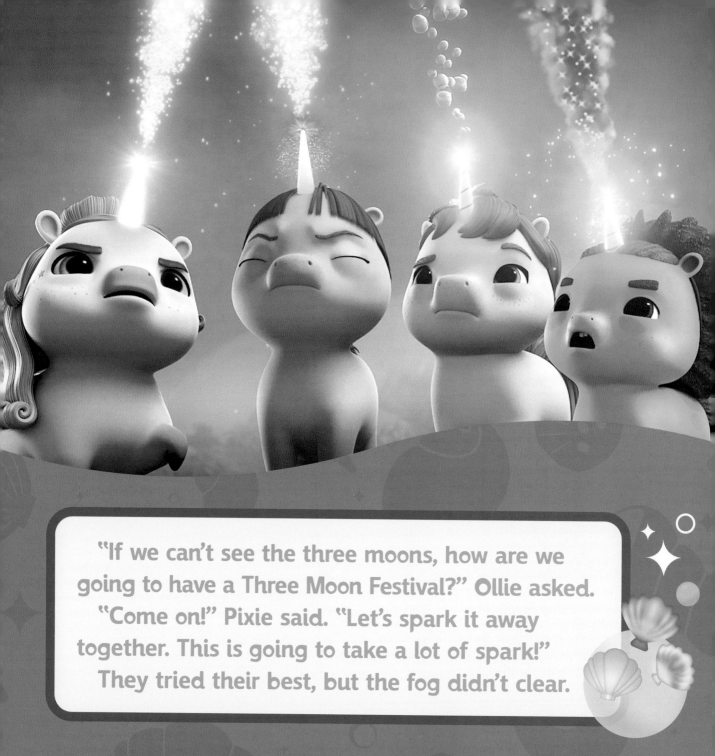

"If we can't see the three moons, how are we going to have a Three Moon Festival?" Ollie asked.

"Come on!" Pixie said. "Let's spark it away together. This is going to take a lot of spark!"

They tried their best, but the fog didn't clear.

Ollie's dad, Chef Jinglehooves, approached. "This fog is so thick," he said. "Too thick for even our Spark to move it. I've never seen anything quite like this before."

"What if we don't move it?" Pixie asked.

"Then the Three Moon Festival will have to be canceled," Chef Jinglehooves said.

"No way!" Ollie cried. "There has to be a way to save the festival!"

"Wait!" Kelp called out.

He suddenly had an idea. "Ollie, during the festival, the sky glows, right?"

"The moons glow. And all the lanterns glow. It's the most glowiest thing you've ever seen!" Ollie looked down sadly. "Except, you won't see it. Because the festival is canceled."

"Maybe not," Kelp said. "Keep decorating for the festival. Juniper, keep practicing your wish lanterns. And when it's nighttime, instead of looking up to the sky, look down to the water."

"But there aren't any moons in the water," Pixie said.

"I don't have time to explain," Kelp said as he galloped away. **"Just trust me!"**

Kelp headed back to the ocean and found Scallop and Cruz.

"How would you like to come to your first Three Moon Festival?" he asked his sea friends.

"Would I ever!" Scallop exclaimed.

"I was hoping you'd ask!" Cruz cheered.

"I've got a plan," Kelp said. "But for it to work, we're going to need a bigger team."

Back on Unicorn Land, Juniper was practicing her wish lanterns.

Meanwhile, the fog was getting thicker.

"We might as well just go home," Ollie said in defeat.

"Kelp has never let us down. So spark up, and levitate that lantern!" Pixie told him. "We've got some wishing to do!"

Back in the ocean Kelp had gathered his friends and family to help. He had an idea of how to use the glowing plankton that was already in the ocean. He hoped his idea would work!

"Kelp!" Scallop cried. "It's almost nighttime at the surface!"

"Follow me, everyone," Kelp told the group. "We'll do our best!"

A few moments later Ollie noticed something in the ocean. "What's that?" he asked.

"The water . . . it's glowing!"

"Is that . . . Kelp?" Pixie asked.
"It is Kelp!" Ollie shouted.

"Those three glowing circles in the water . . . they look just like . . . ," Chef Jinglehooves began.
"Moons!" everyone cheered.

"I'll make my wish to the three water moons!" Juniper told them.

"You can do it! Focus on the three moons," Pixie told her little sister.

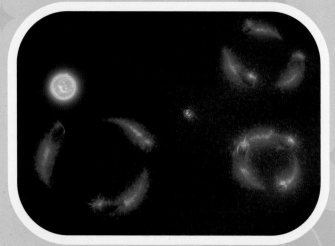

Her wish lantern floated down toward the ocean.

"I did it!" Juniper exclaimed.

"Come on, unicorns!" Pixie announced. "Let's make our wishes!"

Wish lanterns began to float down toward the ocean in circular glittery sparkles! Kelp's mom, dad, and Scallop watched in amazement as the wish lanterns fell into the sea.

"Wow!" Everyone oohed.

Kelp had one last surprise for his unicorn friends.
His family and friends used their blowholes to
shoot glowing water into the night sky!

It was more than any unicorn
expected. They had no idea
narwhals could do that!
"Thank you, Kelp," Ollie said.

"The Three Moon Festival is as amazing as Ollie said it would be," Kelp told Scallop.

"I've never seen anything more magnificent in my entire life," Scallop said dreamily.

"It's time to boogie, boogie, boogie!" Cruz shouted.

They swam to the shoreline and danced with the unicorns.

It was the best Three Moon Festival ever!